I0640853

J. P. Grant

Stray leaves

A collection of poems

J. P. Grant

Stray leaves
A collection of poems

ISBN/EAN: 9783743335127

Manufactured in Europe, USA, Canada, Australia, Japa

Cover: Foto ©Andreas Hilbeck / pixelio.de

Manufactured and distributed by brebook publishing software
(www.brebook.com)

J. P. Grant

Stray leaves

STRAY LEAVES.

A COLLECTION OF

POEMS.

BY

MRS. J. P. GRANT.

Montreal;
PRINTED AND PUBLISHED BY JOHN LOVELL.
1865.

CONTENTS.

PREFACE.

———

S H O U L D you ask me, gentle Reader,—
Very kind and gentle Reader,—
Easy, kind, and soft subscriber
To the volume now before you,
How I came to write this volume,—
What inducement made me print it,—
How I hope to pay the printer !—
I should answer, I should tell you,
In the strain of Hiawatha:
I had not the least intention,
When I penned my modest verses,
That they ever in a volume

Should collected be, and printed;

Printed, prefaced, bound, and published!

Thus it happened:—From my childhood,

Like young Pope, " I lisped in numbers "

(All, I fear, we have in common),

And whene'er occasion prompted,

Slight or weighty, grave or merry,

Birth or burial, christening, wedding,

Sad removal, happy meeting,

Tearful parting, joyous greeting,

Action brave or patriotic,

Faithful love, or warlike daring,

I must have my " lines " upon it,

Venting all my soul in rhyming.

As I grew in years and stature,

Editors my verses welcomed,

Friends around me kindly flatter'd,

Urged me to collect and publish,

Offered to become subscribers,

Offered to procure me others;

Talked of profits, talked of dollars,
(Things I very sadly needed,)
Talked until at last I yielded,—
Vanity, *perhaps*, assisting. ·
Thus it comes to pass, O Reader,
That I throw me on thy mercy,—
Book and author on thy mercy.

Sages tell us that the medium
Through the which we see an object,
Gives it colour bright or glooomy,—
Gives it ugliness or beauty,
Makes it lovely or unlovely ;
Therefore, when thou art perusing
This my unpretending volume,
Read it with the eye of friendship,
Read it by the light of kindness,
Through good-nature's rosiest glasses :
So its unpresuming pages
Shall for thee seem gay with fancy,

Bright with wit and warm with feeling,

Burning with poetic passion,

Glowing with reflected beauty

From thy heart, O gentle Reader!

Thus shall recompense be made thee,

Fair, and good, and manifold,

And thy dollar be repaid thee,

Like a " greenback " turned to gold.

A Legend of Courtney Hall.

———

IT WAS evening—and athwart a grand old room,
 The darkening shadows cast a solemn gloom ;
No tinted twilight breathing peace and rest,
No golden glory lingering in the west,
 But dark and lowering, shutting out the day,
And barricading with black clouds the way,
Whilst angry winds in fitful gusts swept by,
And distant thunder muttered round the sky ;
The tender flowers stood trembling in the gloom,
And the tall poplars waved their hearse-like plumes.
At the carved lattice, two fair maidens stood,
And anxious eyed the distant darkening wood,

With arms entwined, as if or love, or fear,
In close companionship had drawn them near ;—
One, soft and timid, with a shrinking grace,
That from the storm would still avert her face ;
The other, with her dark impassioned eyes,
Seemed scarcely conscious of those threatening skies,
But still gazed onward through the shadows dark
To the small pathway winding through the park :
And when the lightning leapt from out the cloud,
And the torn forest seemed to groan aloud,
When peal on peal, with scarce a moment's space,
Shook the old mansion to its very base,
And Ida, trembling, murmured in dismay :
" Dear Anabel, my sister, come away !"
She turned indeed, but not in fear or dread,
And in a hoarse and shuddering accent said :
" Oh ! Ida, Ida, what the tempest's rage
To the wild warfare that the heart must wage,
When all is staked below, and Heaven above,
On the weak tenure of a human love !

Nature in any aspect seems more fair

Than the low threatenings of that heart's despair.

To-night the shadows of this stifling room

Seem to enclose me in a living tomb ;

Our mother's pictured face upon the wall

No pleasant memories to-night recall,—

Those soft pure eyes seem ever on me bent,

A solemn meaning in their sadness blent ;

And though has passed the sun's last lurid rays,

I still can feel their ever watchful gaze.

Why! I could almost join the vulgar throng,

Who deem our father's wondrous wisdom wrong :—

The science dark, o'er which we see him pore,

Is it indeed, some foul, forbidden lore ?

And are there signs, and influence, and spell,

And awful warnings, who can say or tell ?

No, no! 'tis but the dream, that hideous dream,

That even fled not at the morning's beams,

And, Sancta Maria ! still so real seems—

That now, when I would tell the horror wrung,

A chain seems laid upon my heart and tongue!

But you shall hear it!—Was not that a sigh?

Come nigh sweet sister, ever, ever nigh."

She turned, and locked that soft hand in her own,

And thus continued in half-whispered tone:

" I dreamed, dear Ida, 'twas my wedding morn,—

Perhaps because I think 'twill ne'er be born!—

My spirit, saw myself robed as a bride,

And Herbert standing proudly by my side!

I wore that veil bordered with soft seed pearl,

That Herbert says, makes me a Spanish girl!—

The veil I stole from you long months ago,

Because he praised it, and admired it so!

The Lady Ursel's jewels on my head,

Oh! I would sooner circle it with lead.

What could possess me e'er to dream of them,

But they were there, each sin-accursèd gem;—

I shudder to recall her hideous fate,

Or pass her picture if the hour be late;

For though 'tis veiled, I fancy I can hear

The sound of rustling garments sweeping near;

And e'en our father though sore pressed with need,

For jewels his experiments to speed,

Would rather his life's dream should end in nought,

Than its success by those cursed gems be bought,—

Well—and my veil was down, and on my feet

Were jewelled shoes, and flowers pure and sweet

Lay on my breast—and Herbert, too, he smiled

That buoyant smile that oft my heart beguiled :

Oh! Ida, think you he will still love on,

Still pour the wealth of his dear love on one

So brown and homely. Were I fair like thee,

I could not doubt his fond heart's constancy.

You were not there ; in vain I sought to see

Our father, bridemaids, priests on bended knee ;

The church was empty, silent as a grave,

Though tapers gleamed, and flowers strewed the nave ;

The six great candles on the altar shone,—

Before it I and Herbert stood alone !

I saw him press my hand, and stoop quite near,

Murmuring some sweet assurance in my ear ;

I saw my curls stirred by his perfumed breath,

But all around was still and cold as death !

When lo ! a chasm in the pavement yawned,

And some dread voice from out the chasm warned ;

And when I looked again, all, all were gone,

Bride, bridegroom, altar, flowers, there were none !

Only upon the Lady Ursel's tomb—

Where gaped that chasm, with its awful gloom ;

Lay a few bones, mixed with some jewels old,

And a worn rosary, green and damp with mould !

And then I heard a laugh, distant and low,

And tread of heavy feet far down below !

But what is stranger still, through all the day

The hateful vision will not pass away !

Still I can see those few poor bleached remains,

The gems and rosary still my eye retains,

And still that laugh, those heavy steps I hear

As if of feet carrying an unknown bier.

Heaven shield my Herbert! what a storm, what rain!

He will not come to-night, to hope were vain,

If only I e'er look on him again.

Ida sat still and silent for a space,

Then wistful looked into her sister's face;

" Your fancy, Anabel, is all distrought,

The foolish dream, believe me, it is nought

But this poor feverish pulse that throbs and beats.

I shall call Marion, with her old receipts,—

She shall prescribe—but no ; for only see

Yonder his horse, glancing beneath the tree.

Oh ! Love is swifter than his promise true,

And you must read your omens all anew !

Gently, sweet sister, or that heart will die

Of rapture—ere to calm it he is nigh !

I warrant with such ecstasy elate,

You scarce will tarry till they ope the gate,

And dreams and fears, and all love's fond alarms,

Be quite forgotten in his sheltering arms.

B

Part Second.

Christmas had come—for Time's swift wings had flown,
And in her chamber Ida sat alone,—
Sat gazing in the fire, whose flickering flame
Cast trembling shadows as it went and came ;
Now momentary light in each recess,
And now a pall, with startling suddenness ;
But in the red light glowing softly there,
Ida's transcendent beauty showed more fair !
Her pearly skin, the blush that rose and fell,
As some repressed emotion it would tell,—
Her long and golden hair that floated round
In careless beauty, unadorned, unbound,
Touched by the fitful firelight's pleasant glow,
In shining ripples o'er her shoulders flow !
But who shall tell the glance that light revealed,
Remorse and rapture, both but half concealed ;
The troubled eye, the red lips quivering there,
The soft hands clasped, as if in mute despair ;

A breviary lay forgotten on her knee,

All objects lost in that strange reverie.

Nor did the entrance of her sister seem

To rouse her from that deep bewildering dream !

In truth that maiden's step though firm was light,

And noiseless, as a murderer's in the night.

" We wait," she said, in a deep, quiet tone,

" Your presence now, is all we need alone,

She touched her sister's shoulder, as she spoke,—

Oh what a shudder that slight pressure woke !

And Ida, though her soft frame shrank and shook,

Rose without word, or questioning, or look,

And followed silent, the long corridor,

Till Anabel flung wide a heavy door ;—

But there she paused in fixed and still surprise,

For a strange group met her inquiring eyes.

At a small table in that vast old room,

Lit by a lamp, that scarce could pierce the gloom,

She saw their father, old Sir Courtney, stand,

A parchment trembling in his feeble hand ;

But though in person present on the scene,

To close observer, it might well be seen

His thoughts already from the group had flown

Back to his studies, and his chamber lone.

Another nobleman stood at his side,

Older, and with an aspect differing wide—

Their father, learnèd, visionary wild,

In worldly wisdom simple as a child!

Lord Orde,—if rumour and report spoke true,—

That world, with all its vices, too well knew ;

A saffron coloured, deeply withered cheek,

A small dead greedy eye, with age now weak ;

Lips, that in vain essayed to meet or close

The gumless teeth, would still themselves disclose,

But o'er his shoulders, scented love-locks flowed,

And rare rich gems upon his doublet glowed ;

Whilst on his hands so shrunken, long and lean,

Great costly rings on every joint were seen.

He stood, propped on a staff, curiously wrought,

Some rare sea-monster, from a distance brought,

And had, 'twas said, with a great price been bought.

At the quaint table, 'fore a parchment wide,

With pens and ink-horn ready at his side,

Sat a young scribe, as if, his labour o'er,

He only waited for that opening door,—

And Anabel, with face of livid hue,

Her wondering sister to the table drew,

Dipping a pen in the bronze standish near,

She placed it in her hand, and whispered clear,

Though that low whisper came both harsh and grating :

" Sign, Ida, sign ! you should not keep them waiting!"

And Ida wrote her name in the blank space ;

Her sister's steady finger, marked the place.

Then Anabel one moment seemed to pause,

A spasm sharp, her brow contracts and draws,

She clears it with her hand—the colour came,

Slow and deliberately she traced her name ;

Then old Lord Orde, in cracked discordant tone,

Muttered some tender words, and all was done.

The clerk sealed up the parchment, gathering all,

With his employer left the gloomy hall;

Their father, through the scene, nor spoke, nor stirred,

Rose and retired, without a sign or word.

Anabel turns, as the last footfall dies,—

A vengeful triumph, leaping to her eyes:

" Now, sister, stay—have you no news to break,

No sweet confessions blushingly to make;

Say, shall I speak, or listen first for thine,

Thy tale of love, or [*hissing low*]—or mine."

These biting words, and still more scornful glance,

Seemed to wake Ida from her stony trance,

To plunge her in a passion of wild grief,

That in a storm of weeping, sought relief;

Tears poured like rain, and trembling and distressed,

She would have sunk upon her sister's breast;

But Anabel, with smile and frown forbade,

Both made her shudder and recoil afraid.

" Oh, listen to me, Anabel," she cried;

" Listen and pity ! I will nothing hide;

Poor, weak, distracted, plunged in wretchedness,
Forgive me, sister, I will all confess."
  " Nay, spare yourself the unnecessary pain,
As once you might, dissimulation vain ;
Sister to sister should have spoke out right ;
You should have said, I cannot bear the sight.
Of all your happiness, and love, and wealth,
Into that paradise I'll creep by stealth ;
Fairer than you—with soft and graceful wile
His fickle heart, from you I can beguile.
'Twere a strange speech methinks, but I should know
How to return in kind, the intended blow ;
And *you*, not *I*, been spared the pained surprise,
That, from such want of confidence, must rise,
Ah ! think you I was fooled, nor wit, nor heart,
To avenge the wrong, and baffle your weak art ;
You "—and she laughed with triumph as she spoke,
" Have been yourself a witness to the stroke."
  " Forgive, forgive," murmured her sister fair,
Trembling before the anger blazing there ;

" And 'twas no passion, no wild dream of bliss—
That urged you thus to wreck my happiness,
No aching love, heart-wearing, deep, and true,
That I should talk of love or truth to you ;
I should have spoken of an ancient name,
Broad lands, proud palaces, and beauty's fame.
Well these, spite of your plots, will all be mine,
Then what remains, I calmly can resign ;
And as for bridegroom, matter small, I ween,
If a few years between our age is seen."
Again she laughed, but laugh it did not seem,
More like a lengthened and discordant scream.
" Ah ! you forgot, when you secured the son,
That old Lord Orde, his father, might be won ;
You ne'er conceived, in all you plan and plot,—
And soft cajollery I could counter-plot ;
And when you wrote your name, short time ago,
You ne'er imagined, for you could not know,
That 'twas a marriage contract then you signed,
Between your sister and Lord Orde designed,

In which my dowry, his fond love gift free,

Was his son's disinheritance to be.

Go tell him, he has waited long for you

Under the shade of the long avenue ;

Tell him, as he his love vows would renew,

His bridal morn will be his father's too.

Ah ! I have moved you, and the sharp barb stings,

To-night my triumph and your shame begins."

Ida, whose blood seemed in that storm to freeze,

Now trembling, weeping, sank upon her knees :

" Oh, sister ! at your feet, upon the floor,

By all our girlish love, I beg, implore,

If not for mine, for your own sake, beware,

And this most hideous sacrifice forbear.

Oh ! spare yourself the unutterable shame,

This outrage on your woman's heart and name.

If half unwittingly I've done you wrong,

The barrier, trust me, will not be for long ;

And ah ! how blest, within an early grave,

My woe to hide, and you this horror save."

The short, quick breath, as here she paused a space,

The pleading anguish of that tender face,

The hectic spot on each fair cheek that burned,—

A heart not steeled to pity must have turned ;

But Anabel, with glance of hardened gloom,

Gathering her dress, swept silent from the room.

Part Third.

The spring all delicate, and fair, and young,

Her graceful garlands o'er the earth had flung,

As if unconscious sin and sorrow's gloom

Darkened the world, she clothed with tender bloom.

Or that wild passions lurked within the breasts

To which her blossoms and her blooms were pressed.

Within one house where, but a year ago,

All sweet affections shed perennial glow,

Where happiness and peace, *home* sunshine spread,

Remorse and hatred darkly reigned instead.

Since the sad day when Anabel had signed

The marriage contract that her youth resigned

To drivelling age and sordid lust and power,—

From that despairing, that most fatal hour,

When hope, and love, and confidence were o'er,

The sisters saw each other's face no more.

Ida, who from that day, began to pine,

But left her chamber for the Virgin's shrine ;

Few were the visits, and but short the stay

Of the false lover that she stole away.

Perhaps one, who to his youth's first ardent love,

Could so unfaithful and so fickle prove,

Would tire yet sooner of the love he sought,

When by his wealth and heritage 't was bought.

Daily to Anabel were stories brought,

How Ida, fading, her forgiveness sought ;

How prayed her, not her warning to despise,

And make herself the greater sacrifice.

Such rumours and entreaties were dismissed,

Firm in unholy purpose to persist ;

It seemed as if all softness, feeling, flown,

Her very nature and her heart were stone.

She gathered round her, all most rich and rare,

As if in luxury to lull despair ;

Waiting the day, 'mid pomp and power and ease,

That her consigned to dotage and disease.

Once only was she wavering seen to turn,

Her hand to tremble and her cheek to burn ;

'Twas when Lord Orde's most faithless son had braved

Her stern displeasure, and an audience craved.

She pressed her heart, as if with sudden pain,

Ere she denied him, with a proud disdain ;

No wonder, as the day approached more near,

That Anabel should shrink with sickening fear,

And, as was oft remarked, when wakeful nights

Were the most troubled with the morning's light,

She still new pomps and splendour would devise,

To gild her fate, its horror to disguise.

Thrice had she chose her bridal's rich array,

And thrice, contemptuously, had cast away ;

And when at last was spread before her eyes

The jewelled train, and dress of gorgeous dyes,

She hid her face and, trembling, turned away,

From the rich trappings and the vain display.

But when the maid, struck with this gentler mood

Of her stern mistress, ventured to intrude,

And said, with broken voice and starting tear,

" The Lady Ida's page is waiting here,"—

She answered in a tone brooked no delay,

" Begone, and drive him with the lash away."

Alas ! what strange and fearful change is here—

Muttered the maid—of sorcery, I fear ;

And Lady Ida's soul about to part,—

Good saints above ! she hath a ruthless heart !

Part Fourth.

It was the wedding morn, the fairest day

Of that most blithe and fairest month of May ;

The bride went forth in such a pomp and state,

As Courtney Hall ne'er witnessed, past or late,

Albeit kings had issued from its gate.

But she went forth alone ; for no adept

In pageantry, his room Sir Courtney kept.

And it was whispered, by the maiden throng,

Who bore her train, in pomp and pride along,

The Lady Ida, once so lovely sweet,

Was now too weak to rise upon her feet.

The bride went forth ; and till that bridal hour,

The fulness of her beauty, and its power

Had ne'er been known, or understood, or felt ;

And the eye now, in wonder, on it dwelt,—

Though colour, glance, and step, as she drew nigh,

Made the beholder shrink, fall back, and sigh.

The train was noble, gold in very showers,

The road of triumph, ankle deep in flowers ;

Trumpets and dulcimers before her went,

While thousand eyes were on her beauty bent.

The poor in flocks on every hand were seen

To view the pageantry, not bless its queen ;

And spite of glitter and the gold they fling,

Of sunshine, and the gracious airs of spring,—

Spite of all this, there comes no answering glow,

Men feel the hollow mockery of the show :

And the long bridal train in rich array

Swept on in silence o'er the flower strewn way.

One moment, the long march was stayed, indeed,

By a poor wasted boy, breathless with speed,

Who, the long train, essayed to stay or break,

Entreating, for the Lady Ida's sake,

The ceremony they would yet delay,

If but an hour, entreating them to stay.

But a stout man-at-arms had thrust him back,

And the bride followed her remorseless track ;

Crushing down every thought from gentler powers,

As her small feet seemed trampling down the flowers.

They reached the church ; beside the altar there,

All dressed and perfumed with assiduous care,

Stood old Lord Orde,—the crowd might well deride,

So shrivelled, palsied,—waiting for his bride.

T'was said by some, why, they could scarce divine,

That Anabel, as she approached the shrine,

Had closed her eyes and clenched her fingers tight,

As if to shut some hideous thing from sight.

Others remarked, who saw that hour of gloom,

She placed herself on Lady Ursel's tomb ;

And as she, waiting, stood before the priest,

When music, whispering, and all sound, had ceased,

Was heard far down beneath and under ground,

A low strange, shuddering, and unearthly sound.

But the doomed maiden's jewelled head was bent,

As if unconscious of the dark portent.

And when the church's solemn words began,

No blush was burning, and no tremor ran ;

To each grave adjuration her reply

Was made unfaltering and with steady eye ;

And at its sealed irrevocable close,

The maiden, unassisted, calmly rose :

She e'en submitted, with apparent grace,

To the old bridegroom's skeleton embrace.

There came a pause, the ablest parasite

Among the courtiers, grouped to left and right,

But must recoil from so ill matched a pair,

Afraid to offer gratulations there.

Just as this moment, the poor bleeding page,

Spite of their blows, and the Retainer's rage,

Once more, to pierce the crowded throng essayed,

With resolution not to be gainsayed,

And having reached the aisle, came tottering near

Close to the Lady Orde, and in her ear,

In passionate voice, with his last strength, he said,

" Joy to you, lady—joy to the newly wed,

And this gay throng—the Lady Ida's dead,

And"—as she smiled in doubt with face all pale—

" Here comes Sir Herbert to confirm my tale."

And ghastly as a corpse, Sir Herbert stood,

The gazers looking on, with curdling blood,

For Anabel's wild eyes, were fixed on air,

Or traced his figure, with a vacant stare.

Some thought, that in indomitable pride

She would all knowledge of his presence hide;

Others, that in the moment's hurry, fear,

She really knew not, who it was stood near.

At length her frame began to waver slow,

And in a tone of piercing anguish low,

That oft in fancy, in long after years,

Still rung in her attendants' shrinking ears,

She cried, " Had I but waited, oh too late and vain !"

And sank, half buried, in her gorgeous train.

They raised her awe-struck, trembling, from the floor,

The haughty-hearted Anabel no more,

But a poor frowning, timorous idiot wild,

Upon whose brow bright gems in mockery smiled.

　The long grass now grows thick in Courtney hall,

And ivy clings about its ruined wall.

Night.

T H E night, the great mysterious night,
　　With solemn shadows spread,
A white light touching all below,
　　The white stars over head,
And the pale moon, a phantom fair,
Gliding in silent beauty there.

The busy hum of day is hushed,
　　Whilst in the still profound
Nature's æolian harp begins
　　To tremble, and to sound
As if its thousand whispering strings
Were swept by unseen spirit wings.

And hearts, that through the gairish day,
    But sordid passions knew,
Now seem a *chord* of that great harp,
    To higher influence true,
And swept, and blown on from above,
Answer and thrill with purer love;

Whilst shadows of our buried ones
    Before the vision rise,
Not from the dark graves, where they lie,
    But from the starry skies,
Not cold unanswering as the sod,
But with sweet messages from God.

O holy night! so filled with peace,
    So spiritual and pure,
As if from life's dull work-day toil
    Our spirits thou wouldst lure,
Veiling this hard material sphere
But opening heaven, serene and near.

Modern Love.

HE comes, the maid whose tender soul
　Can cleave to his alone,
The soul—if ancient Bards speak true—
　Once severed from his own;

The maid, that in his boyhood's dreams
　He dimly had discerned;
The maid, for whom in youth's sweet prime
　He evermore had yearned.

Him only can her heart enshrine,
　All other shrines above;
Her only can his charmèd heart
　Love with a perfect love.

She comes, a ray of heavenly light,
　Which, if it beam in vain,
Its happy lustre o'er his life
　May never shine again.

But ah ! pure Love and sweet Romance
　No more their way can win :
The question now the young man asks,
　Is " *Has she got the tin ?*"

Sonnet to my Soul.

WHY art thou sad, my soul—why ever seek
    A solitude, by sorrow only trod ?
  Why pour grief's fountain down my faded
    cheek,
    Why timid shrink beneath afflictions rod ?
Think, there's a time—nor is that time remote
  When toil, and all anxiety shall cease,
Slander, forbear her heart corroding note,
  And sorrow's bleakest storms be hushed to peace.
Yes—there's a time, when free from yearnings vain
  To happier regions, thou shalt joyous rise,
There dwell forever free from grief and pain
  A happy inmate of the blissful skies.
Peace, then, my troubled soul, dismiss thy care,
For all life's blighted hopes are blooming *there*.

The Grave of a Suicide.

WHOSE is that nameless grave, unmarked
    by simple flower or stone,
Why lies it in that dreary spot, desolate and
    alone,
Beneath the frown of those dark trees, whose
    heavy branches fling
Around the dark deserted spot a gloomy shadowing?
Why lies it thus apart from all those little mounds, that seem
Smiling together peacefully, beneath the summer beam?
Oh why is it excluded from the very smile of heaven,
As if to its repose alone no latent hope were given?
That lone grave does not cover one, who in the yellow leaf,
Dropped from the stalk of human life to find in death relief:

Nor hides it one whose infancy became the spoiler's prey,

The bud of promise and of hope, untimely snatched away ;

Nor is it the last home of her, whose lovely pleasant life

Shed happiness and love around—a mother and a wife.

'Tis the memorial of a soul, that perished in its pride,

Of one who dug with her own hands, her grave, and wretched died,

Who recklessly lay down without the hope to Christians
  given

Of wakening from that sleep of death, to happier life in
  heaven,

Unlike the dead whose virtues still by memory are cherished,

Oh truly may we say that her memorial with her perished.

Childhood.

S H O U T, joyous little children,—shout,
    And clap your hands with mirth,
  Send bursts of ringing laughter out
    Over the bright green earth.

On you the angel's nature rests,
    Not yet—not yet 'tis fled ;
Upon your pure and sinless breasts
    Is perfect joy still shed.

Shout, joyous children, shout,—be glad,
    Ere the dark days creep on,
When sounds of mirth seem strange and sad,
    Or like a dream that's gone ;

When your sweet voices shall grow low,
  With sorrow in their tones,
Resembling in their mournful flow
  The wind's deep wailing moans.

Drink of youth's sparkling waters, ere
  Is broke the crystal bowl;   .
Never again such fountain fair
  Shall bless the thirsting soul.

When day is past, calm lights will rise;
  But shine they e'er so bright,
The heart, the weary heart still sighs,
  And feels, alas! tis night.

Thus, when life's glorious morn is past,
  Though many a bliss remain,
Yet pure, unmixed, unclouded joy
  We never taste again.

Charity.

DEAL gently with thy fellow-man,
   However lost—however low;
His inner life thou mayst not scan,
   His bosom's working never know:
Condemn him not—thou canst not tell
How oft temptation he withstood,
From what unguarded height he fell,
   Or what his yearning still for good.

Oh, scorn him not! 'mid passions wild,
   May yet remain some holy spot,—
The treasured memory of a child,
   Or mother's prayer, still unforgot;
Perchance some true, unbroken chord
   May thrill, and vibrate in his heart,
That but a sympathetic word
   To a full heavenly tone might start.

Despise him not—nor e'er despair ;
 Be ours the faith that may not doubt
That the sweet *germ* of good is there,
 Could human eye but trace it out,—
That the dull soil, so hard above,
 Touched by the sunshine and the rain,
Warmed in an atmosphere of love,
 Will yield and soften yet again.

To few, if dark temptations lower,
 The firm and steadfast strength is given
Still to resist the evil power :
 One did it—but He came from Heaven.

And ah ! if He, the pure and true,
 Could hope in every sinner see,
Shall we, who stand, because not tried,
 Forget his God-like charity ?

Earth.

OH pleasant Earth ! still fresh as on the morn
When angels sang for joy that thou wert born,
Thy balmy breath, thy green and dewy sod,
Still fragrant, as if newly come from God,
Thy soft and azure sky, stream, mountain, wood,
Lovely, as when His voice pronounced thee good ;
Sweet native country, of our very soul,
Where first we live, and learn life's heavenly goal,
Where first our spirit, higher spirits feel,
And He the highest, deigns himself reveal,—
Scene of our worthy toil, our hopes and fears,
Bright with our love, and sanctified by tears,

No aliens we, thy sacred breast to tread,

With mingled hate, hostility and dread,

But faithful citzens, that own thy claims,

Pledged by sweet memories to yet higher aims ;

And thou, no place for exiled hellish things,

Usurped by Satan, fanned by baleful wings,

No vengeance in thy happy sunlight burns,

That paints the grass, and fruit to golden turns ;

No threatenings flash from out the starry eyes

That keep their silent watch, from nightly skies,

On thy dear breast, as pure to kneel and pray,

As any pavement in the milky way,

" Holy of holies" now, we seek to see

In what is like, not opposite to thee :

No strain of Heaven, can wake our hearts to prayer,

If thy home music finds no echo there,

And saintly spirits throng around in vain,

If earthly duties unfulfilled remain ;

No stern antagonism may we see

Between thy life, and that which is to be,

Whilst higher states of holiness and bliss

Are but the *sequel* to the plan of this.

Yes, nursery of our souls—loved mother Earth,

'Twas Heavenly Wisdom called thee into birth;

And should that wisdom have decreed the day

When thou in ruin shall be swept away,

'Tis not because thy failure was complete,

Warped from the purpose, that He deemed thee meet,

But that thy course, full well and nobly run,

His plan accomplished, thy long task was done.

Lines To ____

—————

WHEN soft, and still, and peacefully,
　　The shades of evening fall,
　Thy image to my memory
　　How fondly I recall.

But not alone at close of day
　　My thoughts shall dwell with thee,—
　In every moment, sad or gay,
　　Thou 'lt ever present be.

When in my heart is happiness,
　　And pleasure fills mine eye,
　I'll pause amid my joyousness
　　To wish that thou wert nigh.

D

And when my spirits sink, oppressed,
　　Foreboding sorrow near,
Thy image, rising in my breast,
　　Shall check the falling tear.

And when at night, with sweet emotion,
　　To Heaven I bend the knee,
Thou'lt mingle in my deep devotion,
　　And I will pray for thee.

Another Life.

 NOTHER life, another life,
 To heal the wounds of this,
Another life to gather up
 Our shattered dreams of bliss :

Another life to sweep away
 Earth's toil, chimeras, fears,
To shroud the scene where nought is true
 Or permanent, save tears :

Another life—but oh ! so strong
 The chains that bind us here,
We only ask that life, in hopes
 Those dreams will reappear.

The mother craves her erring child,
    Caught in some fatal snare,
She thinks but of his *once* pure eye,
    Her baby's golden hair.

The widow still in anguish seeks
    The lover of her youth;
Remembers not the drunkard's grave,
    But his first vows of truth.

The maiden asks that wondrous light,
    That once such rapture shed,
The youth recalls some fragrant lip,
    Some smile forever fled.

Yes! all demand some treasure lost,
    Some blighted faith restored,
The broken cisterns, into which
    Love was so freely poured.

And was it all poured out in vain,
  Nought but a piteous dream,
Whose very memory must be steeped
  In Lethe's dreary stream?

And is not still that memory
  Sweeter than pictured bliss?
Can any paradise allure,
  Bought at the price of this?

Ah no! but God those broken links
  Will bind, no more to sever,
Can they to the dear Father die,
  Who live to us for ever.

Lines on the Tercentenary of Shakspeare.

DEAR, hallowed shade! so great thy mighty name,

Memorials seem but mockery of thy fame,—

Fame, that shall live untouched by time's decay,

When pyramids in dust are blown away,

No stone, no marble, no insensate thing,

On thy renown can added lustre fling,

But living hearts, warmed by thy spirit's light,

From age to age shall keep thy memory bright.

We live and move beneath the sun's bright blaze,

Nor dream of trophy to record his praise,—

So thy great genius needs no sordid pelf,

Varied, munificent as Nature's self,

That pours forth flower, and herb, and grain, and root,

Scoops lovely valleys at the mountain's foot;

Embosoms in the Ocean's raging breast

Islands that breathe of Paradise and rest.

And over all—the lowly and the grand—

Pours floods of beauty with a lavish hand.

Great, and akin to Nature as thou art,

We can but bring the homage of the heart,—

That heart, whose red leaves thou so well couldst read ;

Its throbbing pulses, and its aching need,

Its love, ambition, ecstasy, despair,—

All the wild passions glowing, seething, there ;

Whose every phase thy hand could bring to view,

Holding " the mirror up to Nature " true.

To day when Nations in their ardour vie,

To celebrate thy birth with pæans high ;

When statesman, poet, orator, and peer,

With holy reverence at thy shrine appear,

Vain and presumptuous seems this weak essay,

But the great subject will embalm the lay ;

And one,—who in thy ever wondrous page,

Could weary toil, or bitter grief assuage,—

One heart, thou still canst elevate and raise,

Here drops its mite of gratitude and praise.

Angels.

THEY say no angels, as of yore,
    Seek our abodes of care;
We entertain them now no more
    All unawares.

Yet well I know one came to me,
    Fresh from the happy skies;
And I too dull to pierce or see
    The thin disguise.

I thought him a dear child of earth,
    Although a gift divine;
And wildly claimed him from his birth
    As mine, all mine.

And busy thoughts, my burning heart
  Would ever more engage,
How he should act a glorious part
  On Life's great stage;

How he should climb the starry heights
  Of science or of song;
Or nobly stem the mighty stream
  Of vice and wrong.

I thought his mission and his fame
  Should spread o'er land and sea;
How could I dream an angel came
  To teach but me?

He left a little grassy mound,
  With hallowed memories here;
He took a wrung, but chastened heart
  Up to a better sphere.

Human Life.

" Are not our days
Days of unsatisfying listlessness ?"—*Shelley.*

HAT! and do all God's precious gifts
But vain and empty prove ?
Shall no true joy the bright eye lift
In happy grateful love ?

Because some little lamp goes out,
Shall we not see the sun—
Despise the pure gems spread about,
If one prove false when won ?

What though some little fount run dry,
Shall we forget free springs—
One false note mar the harmony,
That through the glad earth rings ?

Ah! God be praised, there are true hopes
   That never may take wing;
And flowers of joy in human hearts,
   For ever blossoming:

And there are ever burning lights,
   So warm, and true, and high,
That sin, and death, and sorrow's night
   Their living rays defy:

And there are true and fervid souls,
   Who all his bounties feel,—
Hands that are clasped to thank His love,
   And hearts that grateful kneel.

Lines to a Daughter.

 EAR girl, thou askest me to write,
 And something say of thee;
I do it with sincere delight,—
 Best wishes it shall be.

Perchance, thou mayst be doomed to know
 What sorrow waits on life;
The numerous ills of want and woe,
 And passion's ceaseless strife.

Thou yet mayst have to writhe in pain
 At slander's poisoned tale;
Thou yet mayst suffer pride's disdain,
 And tearful tread life's vale.

But oh! dear child, mayst thou ne'er feel
    Those pangs that conscience brings;
That deadliest grief, howe'er concealed,
    Dread guilt's envenomed sting.

Whate'er thy doom, let open truth
    And innocence be thine;
Let Virtue guide thy early youth,
    To fair Religion's shrine :

There thou wilt find thyself secure,
    As placed upon some rock;
Whence thou canst smile at siren lure,
    Nor fear the billows' shock.

And let this maxim, ever true,
    Sink deep thy soul within;
Few mortals real sorrow knew,
    Till they had first known sin.

Address to the Old Year.

T H O U good old year, linger, oh linger yet!
　How can we see thee part without regret?
Didst thou not bring us gifts of priceless worth—
Joy to the heart, and summer to the earth?
Hast thou not shared in all our hopes and fears,
Witnessed alike bright smiles and secret tears?
Within thy old and withered breast there lies
A world of sweet and sacred memories.
And can we see thee part without regret?
Thou kind old year, linger, oh linger yet!

With thee has many a sunny day been spent;
With thee has mirth, and joy, and song been blent;
Friendship has made thy passing hours all bright;
And love has tinged them with a holier light.

But more than all, thou hast calm seasons brought
Of high resolve, and deep and solemn thought,
When goodness seemed to kneel within the heart,
And supplicate she never might depart.

Yes, precious hours were thine, thou good old year,
And even sorrow makes thee but more dear ;
Whatever blessings may be yet in store,
Thy pleasant face we never shall see more.
Let others hail the advent of the new,
And eagerly its promised joys pursue ;
But I still turn to thee with fond regret :
Thou kind old year ! linger, oh linger yet !

Lines on seeing a Poor Girl reading a Fairy Tale.

O more the toil-worn face is pale :
    Upon her sun-burnt brow
No troubled thought of want or woe
    Is lingering now :
Her youthful heart is far away,
    (Toil, travail, are forgot),
Wandering in golden Fairy-land,
    Where grief is not.

She's dreaming youth's delicious dreams,
    That come alike to all,
Whilst hope, with soft and siren voice,
    Answers her call.
With busy, moving life around,
    She sits entranced and still,
Wrapt in soft magic scenes, that all
    Her senses fill.

Poor toil-doomed dreamer ! must thou wake—
  And must thy spirit sail
Into dull years, when even these
  Sweet visions fail ?
Are youth's bright fancies all the joy
  Thy breast can ever know,
And never stream of real bliss
  That heart o'erflow ?
Not so, not so !   Though dark thy lot,
  Thou child of toil and care,
There is a land, than poet's dream
  More bright and fair,—
A land of pure undying joy,
  Richer than fairy ground ;
Eye hath not seen, nor heart conceived,
  What joys abound :

And its deep peace is not alone
  For rich, and wise, and great,
But every simple, earnest heart
  Of low estate ;

E

Not for the gay and world-renowned,
Who proud on earth have trod ;
But for the meek and poor, who walk
Humbly with God.

Clouds.

ELL me, dear mother, what are clouds,
    So wondrous strange they seem,
Floating across the summer sky
    As noiseless as a dream?

" I watched one rising slowly up,
    Of thick and inky hue,
That over all the landscape fair
    A gloomy shadow threw.

" But as I mourned the sudden change,
    And brightness passed away—
A breeze sprung up, and o'er the cloud
    There glanced a sunny ray.

" And lo ! what seemed so dull before,
  No longer shadow flings,
But, touched with light and glory, turns
  To angel's snowy wings."

" My child," the gentle mother said,
  With a quick starting tear,
" Clouds, both to young and old alike,
  Dark mysteries appear.

" But oh, beloved one! mayst thou still,
  With pure undoubting eyes,
Through earth's dark storms, however wild,
  God's angels recognize."

———•———

DWARD E. was in affluent circumstances, surrounded by friends who admired and esteemed him, not only for the wit and talent with which he was gifted, but what was of infinitely more importance, the sterling qualities of his heart. He had lately married that one only being who alone could make him happy, and she was all that his idolizing love had imagined. With such prospects, who would not have prognosticated for him a long-continued scene of uninterrupted love and happiness; who would not have said, his life will be a bright exception to the general rule, that "man's days are full of evil?" But alas for human hopes and anticipations! Edward E.'s page of prosperity was short, whilst his chapter of adversity proved long and bitter.

Gradually, and by almost imperceptible degrees, he became addicted to the heart-hardening, soul-killing, vice of intemperance. In vain his friends warned, remonstrated, entreated. He either could not, or would not, release himself from the iron grasp of his tenacious enemy. In a few short years he had lost a lucrative situation, was deserted by his warmest friends, and the fate seemed inevitable, that he must eventually fill a drunkard's grave. But there was one gentle being who, unlike all the rest, still remained true to the lost, wretched Edward—one who loved him with that true love "that hopeth all things, believeth all things, that suffereth long, and is kind." It was his own meek, uncomplaining wife, who thus hoped, thus believed. She had again and again been entreated to return to her father's house, where she could again enjoy those comforts and luxuries to which from her youth she had been accustomed: but what to Mary was comfort and luxury without him who alone formed her happiness? "No," she would reply to all their persuasions; " am I not his own wedded wife? have I not sworn to love him through everything, and Edward will yet be reclaimed,

I know he will!" And oh! blessings on that fond, trusting woman's heart! Edward was at length reclaimed, and through her gentle influence and instrumentality. True, she had to go through long years of humiliation and suffering; true, she had to endure poverty, pride's neglect, and the world's scorn, but it was for his dear sake; and God, who holds in His hands the hearts of men, had prepared for her a rich reward, even the consummation of that for which alone she lived.

It was a dark, rainy night in November. In an upper apartment of a small house, situated in the suburbs of the town, sat Mary—still lovely, though the bright bloom of health seemed to have faded forever from her fair young cheek. The room was poorly furnished, but scrupulously clean and neat; a small fire burned cheerfully in the grate, and on a table placed near it was a scanty supper, apparently for one. Mary was seated near a cradle, which ever and anon, as its little inhabitant moved, she would bend over or rock with her foot. She had been for some time absorbed in deep, and it would seem, troubled thought, for as she gazed in the fire, a large tear had gathered in her eye, and hung heavy on the

long dark lash. " I am afraid he will not come," at length
she murmured ; "and yet he promised so faithfully he would."
Mary sank upon her knees ; her lips moved not in prayer,
but there was more of beseeching, imploring earnestness in
those raised eyes than any language could have expressed.
At that moment a low knock was heard at the street door.
Mary sprang up, rushed to the top of the stairs, and stood
leaning eagerly forward to catch the first sound ; it was
indeed his voice, and the step seemed steady as it ascended :
she returned to the room and stood leaning against the wall
for support. Edward entered, not with his usual flushed face,
unsteady gait, and excited manner,—his face was animated,
it is true, but it was the animation of an approving conscience,
and the consciousness of having gained a greater victory
than earth's conquerors ever achieved—namely, a victory over
himself and the demon of intemperance. He advanced to
Mary ; and, placing his arm round her waist, he began, " My
own Mary"—and his voice was soft and low, and to her ear
as musical as in happy years long since flown — " my
own Mary," he went on, " my guardian angel, whose love has

been a sweet unquenchable light in my dark path of sin and degradation, ever alluring me back to virtue, let this"—and as he spoke he placed the temperance pledge in her hand,—"which I have this night signed, and which, with God's blessing, I hope to keep, be to us a pledge of returning happiness." Oh who can paint the love, joy, gratitude, that leaped into those late melancholy eyes, or the bright blood that suddenly crimsoned cheek, neck, brow, and as quickly ebbed back to her too happy heart, as she hid her face in his throbbing breast and wept aloud!

Edward E——, is now a doting husband, an affectionate father, a steady, industrious man, and I have no doubt, will soon be a prosperous one. For " I have been young, and am now old, yet have I never seen the righteous man forsaken, or his seed begging their bread."

Home.

WHEN evening flings her dusky shade
  O'er day's departing close,
When labour drops the pen or spade,
  For pleasure or repose,
With hasty step, and gladsome heart,
  I seek my much loved home,—
A cot that boasts no builder's art,
  An unaspiring dome.

Yet here the virtues, with their train
  Of social joys, resort,
Here health, and peace, and freedom reign,
  Fair exiles from a court.

When heard my swift approaching feet,
　　What transports stir within ;
Affection tunes her welcome sweet,
　　A happy joyous din.

My children spring to share my kiss,
　　A lovely, smiling group;
Here centred is a mother's bliss,
　　And all a father's hope.
My loving partner, in her turn,
　　Anticipates desire ;
And oft, as if it would not burn,
　　She trims the kindling fire.

And round that warm, and smiling hearth,
　　How sweet the moments glide ;
Converse and books, and song, and mirth,
　　The happy hours divide.

As thus continual pleasures rise,

    To gild my dear abode,

To Heaven I lift my grateful eyes,

    And thank a bounteous God.

Lines to Fanny.

EACE rest upon thee, lovely one;
  Around thy sunny way,
Spring flowers of happiness alone,
  Ne'er to decay.

Far, far from Fanny's gentle breast
  Be sorrow's withering blight;
The gloom of woe-destroying rest,
        Misfortune's night.

Unknown to her the bitter sigh,
  The sadly aching heart;
The tears that, to the mournful eye,
        Unbidden start.

Her fairy dreams of early youth,
   O let not time destroy ;
Hope's whispers be the voice of truth,
          Foretelling joy.

All sweet affections may she know,
   Fair friendship's ray divine ;
And love's more fervent, holy glow,
          Around her shrine.

Her cup of happiness be full,
   Whilst on her gentle brow
May peace sit ever beautiful
          And fair as now.

Farewell to the Flowers.

FAREWELL, sweet flowers, farewell!
 Your brief, bright reign, is past,
And the heart sighs the old regret,
 O'er joy that may not last—

Sighs that for all that's beautiful,
 But one sad emblem's found;
The grass that flourishes to-day,
 To-morrow strews the ground.

Farewell! sweet, smiling summer days—
 " Ethereal softness " fled;
How loath the heart to link thee with
 The lost—the past—the dead!

And yet, sweet evanescent gems,
　　Your mission was not vain;
In thousand hearts your beauty woke,
　　Thoughts that will still remain.

When Jesus spoke, how short the space
　　His accents thrilled the air;
And yet what everlastingness
　　In every word was there!

A few low sounds in Galilee,
　　Long centuries ago,
Are echoing still o'er all the earth,
　　And shall for ever flow.

And so your beauty, summer flowers,
　　When summer days depart,
Still leave their pleasant memory
　　To linger in the heart.

And when we only hear His voice
    In wintry storm and hail,
We'll think how late He spoke in flowers,
    Nor doubt His love can fail.

F

Lines on the Opening of a Church.

WHAT altar could we raise, O God!
    What temple worthy thee ?
Is not the whole adornèd earth
    Thy holy sanctuary ?

Are not the portals of the east
    Its wide and lofty door ;
And field, and stream, and sun, and shade,
    Its tessellated floor ?

The crimson clouds that float at eve,
    A gorgeous drapery spread ;
And sun and moon, thy golden lamps,
    Undying lustre shed.

And yet, Great God, Eternal One,
　　Inhabiting all space,
Wilt thou thy special presence deign,
　　To bless this humble place ?

Here may the yearning spirit hold
　　Sweet intercourse with Thee ;
And here the meek and contrite find
　　Thy mercy full and free.

Here let the high resolve be made,—
　　The song of praise ascend ;
And in the prayer of earnest love,
　　Spirit with spirit blend.

Here let us sit at Jesus' feet,
　　The way, the truth to learn ;
Whilst, as of old, at that loved voice,
　　" Our hearts within us burn."

And when at length these walls decay,
Grant, for His sake divine,
We may have joined that blessed church
Which is for ever Thine.

Moonlight.

————◆————

IS sweet to watch the Queen of night
  Wade through the stormy sky,
Vapours and mist obscure her light—
  Clouds on her pathway lie.

Yet calmly she pursues her course,
  'Mid all their dark array;
With firm, untiring, gentle force,
  She braves the troubled way.

Image of patient virtue, firm,
  Life's duties to fulfil,
Treading truth's high and holy path,
  Through good report and ill;

Having within herself a power—
A pure and heavenly light—
That calumny and sorrow's hour,
   May hide, but cannot blight ;

That yet shall stream through endless sky,
   Shall onward fearless move,
Radiant with immortality,
   And holy faith and love.

Affliction.

FFLICTION solemn, dark and dread,
Why dost thou haunt the paths we tread,—
Why, with a stern persistent malice,
Press to our lips thy nauseous chalice ?
Were not humanity more blest,
If sorrow could not tear the breast,
If cold indifference e'er reigned,
If grief ne'er stung nor pity pained,—
Would not that soul most happy be,
Who, upon pleading misery,
Could look without a sigh or tear,
Callous alike to grief or fear ?
Ah, no ! thou dark-robed angel, no !
Better to drain thy cup of woe,

Better thy most envenomed dart,

Than thus to ossify the heart.

Softened and moved, the anguish deep

Leads us to " weep with those that weep,"

Whilst virtues, that in day ne'er bloom,

Shed in thy night a rich perfume.

But more than all, dark shade! 'twas thine,

To wake the Poet's art divine ;

He learned, beneath thy rugged sway,

To pour his sorrows in the lay,

And as more keen he felt thy goad,

The tender note more sweetly flowed ;

Refined by thee, e'en grief could please,

And from the tear-drop he extracted ease.

Christmas Hymn.

———•———

UPON Judea's wide-spread plains,
  Midnight and silence hung ;
O'er palm and stream, and olive grove,
  The stars soft radiance flung ;
Whilst gentle flocks at rest appear,
Watched by the Syrian Shepherds near.

When lo ! what brightly flashing light
  Above the scene is spread,
Now glancing o'er the distant hills,
  Now o'er the Shepherds' head !
It is some glorious meteor born,
Or golden beams of coming morn !

Hark! what celestial breathing strains
    Fall softly on the ear ;
The clouds roll back, angelic forms,
    Bending above, appear,
Whilst swells the sweet triumphant hymn
Of Cherub and of Seraphim.

" Peace, peace on earth !" the angels sung
    Long centuries ago ;
Yet still the sword our Saviour sheathed
    Is steeped in blood and woe !
Still wars and strife and tears remain :
Was the sweet Anthem sung in vain ?

Oh ! come, thou Prince of love and peace,
    Assert thy righteous sway ;
Oh ! come, thou kingdom of our God,
    For which we daily pray !
Ages of peace predicted long,
Dawn on our world of strife and wrong.

The Prince of Wales

WHILE ON HIS VISIT TO CANADA.

O palaces, " no cloud-capt towers,"
No antique fanes are here,
No serried ranks of martial powers,
No proud star-breasted peer.

No poet with a lip of fire—
No orator divine,
And yet, thou well-beloved Prince,
No welcome grand as thine.

Rivers that sweep o'er half a world,
   Shall proudly bear thee on,
The harmony of cataracts,
   Thy grand triumphal song.

Primeval forests, open wide,
   A broad and proud highway,
Yielding their ancient, solemn realm,
   To Briton's mightier sway.

Whilst skies all glorious as the scope,
   Of Empire they embrace,
And blue as Saxon's maiden's eyes,
   Thy youthful presence grace.

And gifts whose priceless worth surpass
   Rich argosies at sea—
Or all the gems of all the mines,
   Our shores shall proffer thee !

Thousands of hearts resolved and true,
  Hands ready and prepared!
Old England's bidding well to do,
  Her sacred throne to guard!

"Ich Dien!" serve only right, young Prince;
  God grant the world may see
A mother's and a nation's prayers
  Richly fulfilled in thee!

Footprints of Christ.

———•———

It is a tradition of the early Catholic ages that, a chapel being built on
the spot from which Christ ascended, it was found impossible either
to pave the place on which he last stood, and where the marks of
his feet remained, or to close the roof over that place, and which
was the path of his ascent.]

I S an old legend, and though born
    In superstition's night,
Its import's beautiful and true
    To those who read it right.

For the dear footprints of our Lord,
    Nor time nor art efface ;
Still over earth's dark wilderness
    His glorious steps we trace.

And the bright path of his ascent
    Into the peaceful skies,—
Oh ! what shall veil it to our hope,
    Or close it from our eyes.

Life has wild tracts where we should sink
    In anguish and dismay,
Had not His patient footsteps passed,
    And sanctified the way.

And death ! Before its portals dark,
    How should we trembling stand,
Did not that glorious path reveal
    Jesus at God's right hand.

O, blessed Saviour ! tender guide,—
    Humanity's sweet friend ;
In life or death thou, only thou
    Canst solace or defend.

England.

———•———

T H O U glorious land ! whose very name
Wakens a proud exultant flame,
Swaying from thy small island space,
The destinies of all the race,
Scattering the seeds of empires vast,
On shores undreamed of in the past,
Leaving memorials of thy hand
On every sea and every land,—
Thou classic ground of liberty,
Where mind and body both are free,
School of all science, knowledge, song,
Mart of all trade where nations throng ;
Before whose arms, victorious, proud,
Wrong and oppression ever bowed.

Enthroned on thy fair island home,

Greater than once imperial Rome :

For should thy sceptre pass away,

Thy power and freedom know decay ;

Should the brave hearts that rule the waves,

Degenerate to timid slaves ;

Thy cities, ruins of the past,

Thy river of ten thousand masts,

A solitary stream that wets

Some naked fisher's drifting nets,—

Were these annihilated, yet

Thy sun of glory could not set.

Wherever meets a faithful band,

In freedom's cause to make a stand ;

Where'er the martyr spirit burns,

And intellectual slavery spurns,—

There thy great spirit still will lead

To noble thought and mighty deed.

Where'er, by solitary lamp,

In chamber lone, or dungeon damp,

Science still works, or bears the brand
Inflicted by the bigot's hand,—
Thy influence shall waken there,
The zeal to toil, the strength to bear.
And oh! where literature consoles,
From the meridian to the poles ;
Where'er it soothes the grief and fears
Of hearts that fail with wakeful tears,
Or brings a joy to eyes that weep
For the dark house and the long sleep,—
There shall thy Spensers, Shakspeares rise,
Thy Miltons sing of Paradise,
And there, in rich and noblest form,
Thy soul shall bless thy genius warm.

Fresh in eternal youth, dear land,
Thy glory shall forever stand,
Thy power, thy mission, thy control,
Imperishable as the soul.

Eden.

H, there are times when the worn heart,
  Weary and tempest-tossed,
Will pause amidst life's pain and strife
  To mourn on Eden lost.

Tired of tumult, sick of guilt,
  Wounded in hope and love ;
Trembling in faith, it eager asks
  The swift wings of the dove,

To bear it to some happier sphere,
  Some safer home than this—
Weeps, wildly weeps, lost Paradise,
  With all its tranquil bliss.

And we will weep,—but yet again
   Renew our mighty powers ;
An Eden's happiness is poor,
   To what may yet be ours,—

The happiness of virtuous deeds,
   The moral victory gained ;
The fight, the race, the glorious crown,
   The heaven to be attained.

Yes, sweet was Eden's vernal air,
   Its rose without a thorn,
Its shady bowers, its tranquil joys,
   Of innocency born.

But sweeter far, when trial o'er,
   And the long race is run,
To hear the Master's voice proclaim,
   " Faithful and true, well done."

"He Tempers the Wind."

U P O N the hard and sterile rock
   The velvet moss still clings ;
Around the naked ruin's wall
   The ivy beauty flings.

Clasping the bare and blasted oak,
   The mistletoe is found ;
And pine and cedar flourish fair,
   When all is dead around.

And, God be praised ! the human heart,
   When wrapt in sorrow's gloom,
Still finds some tender tie to life,
   Some gourd with sudden bloom.

Love's deathless tendrils still will twine
    Its ruined arches o'er,
Cover the wounds they may not heal,
    Its broken shrines restore.

Yes, none so desolate and lost,
    But still on earth will find
That to the shorn and trembling lamb
    " He tempers the rough wind."

Lines.

WEEP not now, as once I wept,
   Nor breathe the frantic prayer
That the same pall that covered him
   Might shelter my despair.

Too *saintly* now my lost one seems,
   For him such grief to pour ;
And if the yearning heart still bleeds,
   Its bitterness is o'er.

At first my darling disappeared
   In darkness and in night ;
But now I know 't was blinding tears
   That hid him from my sight.

And, as I wipe those tears away,
 And through the years look back,
A vanished angel he appears,
 Leaving a shining track,—

A shining track, that through life's skies,
 By cloud or tempest rent,
Smiling and peaceful still points on
 The way my treasure went.

Stars.

YE holy and unchanging stars,
　　Like fond eyes o'er me bent,
　Watching with looks of love afar,
　　Silent, yet eloquent,—

　Are your bright orbs, soft shining there,
　　Seen e'en by mortal eye,
　Those future realms of beauty, where
　　Sorrow and sadness die ?

　Are ye indeed that land where joys
　　In copious torrents roll,
　Where love, without one dark alloy,
　　Can satisfy the soul,—

That land where pleasures, as they fly,
    On golden harps are hymned,
Where blissful bosoms never sigh,
    Where eyes are never dimmed ?

Oh, thrilling thought ! my heart would rise,
    Would leave this heavy clay,
Yearning to spring to those calm skies,
    Where our beloved stay.

But no : enough that unto me
    The blessed boon is given,
On this dark pilgrimage, to see
    Glimpses of their bright heaven ;—

Enough to know the stars of night,
    Whate'er their orbs may be,
Are, O my God, sweet beacon lights
    To point us unto thee,—

To feel assured that thou wilt still
  Some blessed place prepare,
Where all, who humbly do thy will,
  Shall meet in rapture there.

Canadian Amusements.

.

Sleighing.

TALK of Venus reclined in her pearl-gleaming
shell,
Borne gracefully on by the ocean's proud swell,
Shedding rapture and glow o'er the foamy sea,—
No doubt 'twas a picture delightful to see.
But ah! there is one both sweeter and dearer,
And at all events it is very much nearer ;
'Tis our own charming girls, fresh, lovely, and gay,
Reclining with us in the ermine-lined sleigh ;
Gliding along through the feathery snow,
The bells, like her laugh, ringing sweet as we go,

Whilst veiling her face, and her bright sunny glance,

Soft clouds, as in heaven, her beauty enhance.

Old winter may storm, but the heart cannot freeze,

If we only may figure in pictures like these.

Skating.

'Mid varied joys, the Skating Rink behold,

The scene of pleasure yet unsung, untold ;

Here youthful hearts in merry concord meet,

To chase old winter with their flying feet ;

Here gay flirtations, innocent and bright,

Unmixed with envy, gossiping, or spite.

See the young beauty, in her flying grace,

Challenge and tempt the lover to a race :

With streaming hair, and coral lips apart,

The fairy vision still before him darts.

Like Atalanta, skimming o'er the plain,

He follows fast, but follows her in vain.

No time for words—but flashing eyes can speak,—

Victorious roses flame across her cheek:

Eager she bends—already in her soul

She seems to touch the anticipated goal,—

One moment here, another she is gone !

Makes one grand curve, approaches like a swan,

Takes his strong hand, and, glancing, seems to say,

" Just such the race I'll lead you some fine day !"

Snow - Shoeing.

Tramping fearless, forth we go

Over the pathless wilds of snow—

Over the billowy ridges white,

Scaling the mountain's towering height ;

Where human foot could never dare,

We leave the track of our snow-shoe there,—

A track that, seen in later age,

Would puzzle sore the wisest sage.

How geology would be stirred,—

Was it a beast, or was it a bird?

Whilst some Cuvier would declare,

After much research and care,

He thought it the seat of a cane-bottom chair,—

But why at measured distance placed,

Or why the mountain top it graced,

He 'd leave by others to be traced.

But what care we for sages' lore ;

Tramping light, the snow drifts o'er,

Our stainless path all dazzling white,

Flinging back the sunbeams' light,

Whilst piled up clouds of mimic snow

Seem resting on the earth below,—

Or, like huge icebergs sailing slow,

Across the sky's blue depths they go,

To interpose their giant form

Between us and the sunbeam warm.

But cloud, nor cold, nor storm, can damp

The merry heart on snow-shoe tramp :

The only evil we can know

Is meeting with an overthrow ;

For oh ! the struggle long and vain

To get upon one's legs again ;

And as misfortune's cup you quaff,

To hear the world's unfeeling laugh!

But e'en this pang we soon console

In another warmer bowl,

When the merry tramp is ended

Sugar, whiskey, lemon blended,

With song, and mirth, and genial smiles

We loose the straps, and boast the miles.

Tobogging.

Tobogging with frolic rife,

Type of the ups and downs of life,

The easy sloping, slippery plain,

The toilsome marching up again,

Man still, as ever, bound to steer

The lady with a secret fear.

Long endless centuries have run

Since Phaeton tried to guide the sun,

Since with the flaming car of day,

The immortal coursers ran away.

The world was saved from wreck and fire;

But what can quench the wild desire

That still in every man remains

To seize the whip and grasp the reins,

Still the ambition of his life,

To rule his horses, or his wife.

But see them now about to start,—

She, with her trembling fluttering heart,

Heroically hides the fear

That ever makes her cling more near.

In the mean time he, with no notion

Of immolation or devotion,

Begins to set the bark in motion,

Ready with outstretched guiding foot,

The lady with her eyes tight shut,

H

Poised for one moment o'er the steep,

Down which the next, they headlong sweep.

As some proud ship, slips from the stocks,

Glides swiftly, without jars or shocks,

Rushing to find her realm and rest

Upon the waters' heaving breast,

So they as light and graceful sweep,

To find the plain as she the deep.

And now in triumph they return,

Her recent fears, the fair one spurns,

Whilst guiding this small craft aright,

Has only whet his appetite ;

So, as they mount the steep ascent,

He hints, how well he'd be content

To take so sweet a freight in tow,

Not for one hour, and through the snow,

But through a life long voyage, all bright

With love's young dream and warm delight,

Scouting the thought of wreak or fear,

With her to bless, and he to steer.

"Look not upon the Wine when it is Red."

———◆———

TELL me not wine, with its ruby light,
    Will increase our love, our mirth;
To me it speaks of affection's blight,
    And the desolated hearth.

Say not each bubble that springs to the top,
    Is a spirit of social glee;
To me it emblems the sad tear-drop
    On the cheek of misery.

And the spirits round that festive board,
    To me are a ghastly host;
Silent they enter and take their seats
    Like the murdered Banquo's ghost.

There are hoary heads, bowed down with care,
    That on tender filial breasts,
Honored, and peacefully pillowed there,
    Should have sunk to holy rest.

There are children, such as Jesus loved,
    Squalid, neglected, and wan,
No sunny light in their eyes or hair,
    " Of such is the kingdom "—gone;

And women, hardened, and coarse and lost,
    All vestige of womanhood dead;
Once tender as those who clasped the cross,
    From which man, dismayed, had fled;

And youth, with its energy, power, and light,
    But its glorious promise o'er;
On every promise and gift a blight,
    More deadly than leper's sore.

And 'mid the toast and jingling glass,
   Their groans and sighs seem deeper ;
And vain, and vain, the Cain-like thought,
   " Am I my brother's keeper ?"

For in every blighted, wasted life,
   In each anguished face I scan,
There breathes the prophet's awful words,
   " Thou art the very man."

On the Death of H. F. C.

Is it not more beautiful for the young cheek to be blanched by death than life ?—*From the German of Richter.*

NOT yet the summer's bloom is o'er,
Not yet the rose has fled,
But oh! a brighter, dearer spring,
A sweeter flower is dead.

Why wert thou given to the earth,
To blossom for a day,
And then in all thy loveliness
Untimely snatched away ?

Still, still to catch thy graceful form,
    In many a scene we turn
And start from yearning dreams of thee,
    Alas, to clasp thy urn !

Yet thou art happy, blessed child,
    In thy fresh bloom to die,
To carry that pure gentle heart,
    Untainted, to the sky,—

To pass from youth's unclouded scene
    To regions yet more fair,—
From bright, but fleeting joy below,
    To bliss eternal there.

Spared the dark pilgrimage of life,
    Untouched by grief or sin,
'T was easy, thou beloved one,
    For thee to 'enter in.'

But ours the danger, ours the loss,
   To work and to endure,—
To make, with fear and trembling,
   Our own election sure.

If in this cold, ungenial clime
   For thee to die was gain,
Yet darker, lonelier is the path
   To those that must remain.

But we will take thy angel life
   As a sweet holy spell,
For nought but pure and peaceful thoughts
   Can with that memory dwell.

Trees.

T H E trees, the trees, the beautiful trees,
  Waving about in the summer breeze,
Some tossing proud like a warrior's plume,
Some sweeping low, o'er that warrior's tomb,
Some trailing their pendent branches green,
With gothic arches traced between ;
Some spreading vistas of green arcades
Peopled by poet with dryad or maids ;
Some swaying dark, majestic and slow,
Some dancing in breezy mirth below,—
All in their graceful foliage drest,
Waving or dancing, but never at rest.

The trees, the trees, the colourless trees,

Stiff and stark in the wintry breeze,

Bare in their winding sheets of snow,

Shrouding the lifeless forms below,

Each outstretched branch and twig defined

Sharp on the leaden sky behind,

And all around, a cold still breath,

Thrilling the heart, like a thought of death,—

Death, in its still impassive form,

No trembling now to breeze or storm,

No graceful swaying, to and fro,

The south may kiss, or the north wind blow ;

Even the sunshine no life can bring,—

They wait, like the dead, for another spring.

The trees, the trees, the colourless trees,

Stark and stiff in the wintry breeze.

The Man of Leisure.

———•———

"OH, please, sir," said a pale, thin boy,
  "Please, did you get the place?"
And as he spoke, an eager light
  Flashed o'er the poor, wan face.

"Why, no," the man of leisure said,
  "But you shall have it soon;
Perhaps, about it, I'll drop in
  This very afternoon."

Time sped; the man of leisure dined
  After a solemn grace;
Again was heard the painful voice,
  "Please, did you get the place?"

" Why, no," the man of leisure cried;
    " How could I so forget?
I'll see about it, my poor boy,
    And you shall have it yet."

Long weeks wore on, the pale boy stood
    Brushing a glossy coat;
A deeper shadow in his eye
    The man of leisure smote.

" Oh, I must really stir myself,
    And see about that place."
No sickly light of " hope deferred"
    Now flashes o'er the face.

The poor lip quivers, tears gushed forth;
    With choking voice he said,
" Oh, please, sir, never mind it now,
    For mother, sir, is dead."

The United States.

— • —

HE spirit of the Pilgrim Fathers wakes
At freedom's call; its lengthened slumber
breaks;
Again the latent energy has blazed,
That in a wilderness an empire raised,
Which though to exile and to death resigned,
Would brook no fetters on the free-born mind.
That spirit, that a Washington inspired,
And 'gainst oppression a whole nation fired;
That spirit that awakes the lofty trust,
" Thrice is he armed who hath his quarrel just ;—
That glorious spirit once again prevails,
And dark oppression's bristling front assails:
On Southern arrogance its hand is laid;
Its voice bids slavery's bloody waves be stayed.

Once more the great Republic rises, proud,

Freed from the curse 'neath which she long had bow'd,

That made her blush, the butt of every sneer,

Her shame abroad, her degradation near ;

Sternly resolving to assert the power,

To give to all her children man's best dower,

For the great struggle, summoning her best,

With their life's blood, her honour to attest ;

Steeping her soil in blood, and tears, and strife,

But, in return, bestowing more than life,—

The promise of a flag without a blot ;

Expunged forever slavery's damning spot ;

And like the land from whence her children spring,

From weeping slaves the cursèd shackles fling.

For such an end, and in his country's cause,

What heart so dastard as to stand or pause ?

Who would not spring all ardent to oppose

His glowing breast a bulwark to her foes,

Deeming for her no sacrifice a pain,

No death untimely, and no offering vain ?

The Modern Young Man.

HE modern young man is a puzzle, a wonder,
E'en Cupid himself is obliged to " knock under ;"
Now only presuming to level his dart
At woman's more soft and susceptible heart.
He will flirt in a charming indefinite way,
But to really make love, why the thing " would not pay ;"
If he talks of himself, or tells you a story,
'Tis not, as of old, about honour and glory ;
Not of hunting, or shooting, or danger to seek,
But how many dollars he made in a week ;
Not cricket, or boating, or wit at the board,
But how close o'er the leaves of his ledger he poured.
If you talk of a girl as pretty and good,
He asks if her fortune is well understood ;

What her station in fashion's ricketty scale,

If her uncle or brother last year did not fail.

Should you hint in *herself* a rich fortune he'd win,

He says, " 'Tis no go," and " you can't take him in."

Speak of children as sun-beams that spring-time renew,

In the darkest of storms their sweet light glistening through,

He vows, " olive branches, if valued of yore,

Are now below par and a deuce of a bore."

Should you ask has he seen the latest Review,

He tells you " he's something better to do ;"

That literature some people's joys may enhance,

But that he keeps his eye upon the " main chance."

He boasts " that his faith in most things is small ;

His belief is in figures—and that's about all.

All generous affections seem withered and dead,

His heart has turned grey ere the locks on his head ;

For the follies of youth, he has not enough fire

To make them temptations, or kindle desire ;

Whilst still in his mind a fear's lurking dim

That all the *fair sex* have designs upon him

So he makes them clearly and well understand

'Twould be useless to hope or to sue for his hand.

Oh, well may the girls their lost empire deplore !

And sigh for the chivalrous days of yore,

When a man was a man—warm, daring and bold,

Who imperilled his soul for *her* love—not for gold.

Who, whatever his blunders in thought, word, or deed,

Made love his religion, and woman his creed ;

Who thought it the aim of his turbulent life

To adore the whole sex, and *take one for a wife.*

I

Hope.

I N each scene of man's life to age from a child,

Not to have but to hope is his doom;

He pursues a vain phantom that ever beguiles,

And sighs for the joys yet to come.

In boyhood, though happy, he still will complain,

And look with disgust at the ferrule and sum,

He longs to be freed from the pedagogue's chain,

And sighs for the joys yet to come.

In the fair spring of youth, in the morning of life,

When each pleasure presents its first bloom,

He looks forward to manhood, the babe, and the wife,

And sighs for the joys yet to come.

But life has its trials, it is not all fair ;
    Each day brings its struggle or gloom :
He pictures old age free from from toil in its chair,
    And sighs for the joys yet to come.

Yet age has its cares ; the pleasures all fly,
    And nought now remains but the tomb ;
Still hope with sweet solace points up to the sky,
    And sighs for the joys yet to come.

Bella.

BELLA, with the summer's dawn
    Upon her blushing cheek;
Bella, with its tender starlight
    In her eyes so meek.

Bella, with the lights and shadows
    Flitting through her breast;
Ecstasies and tender dreaming,
    Undefined, yet blest.

Bella, simple, sweet, and calm,
    In her maiden grace;
Yet impassioned prophecies
    Mantling o'er her face.

Bella, with her future path
　Like a landscape fair,
Knows not of the hidden graves,
　Flower-covered there,—

Knows not of the wintry blast
　Or the sun's eclipse ;
Dreams not darker smiles than her's
　Part the trembling lips.

May the darling never know
　Aught of grief or sin ;
Calm be her pilgrimage below,
　And sweet the " *enter in*."

Lines on the Death of an Only Son.

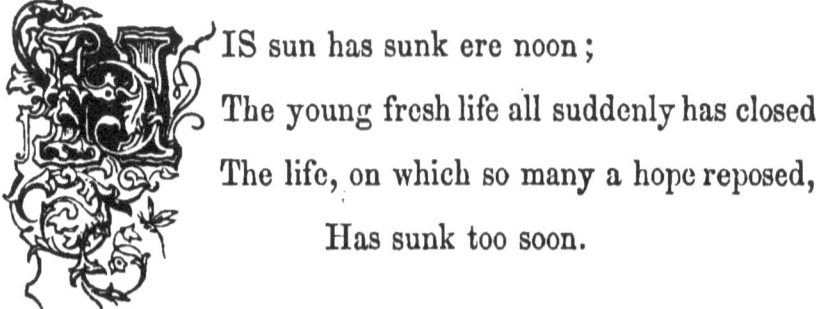

IS sun has sunk ere noon;

The young fresh life all suddenly has closed.

The life, on which so many a hope reposed,

Has sunk too soon.

Too soon, too soon, we say,

If we take counsel only with the heart,

That clings so wildly to the outward part,—

The earthly clay.

Too soon, if we demand

The sweet continuance of those tender ties,—

The living light, that shone in those closed eyes,

The clasping hand.

Too soon, if we recall
The earthly promises that life contained,
The noble possibilities that waned
    Beneath his pall.

But not too soon when seen
From a serener and a higher plane,
When the soul's vision reaches him again,
    No tears between.

When through our grief, at last,
We can perceive the shining golden shore,
Death but the prelude, and the opening door
    Through which he passed.

What, though he passed ere noon!
The Reaper found him for the harvest mete,
No ravelled shapeless life, though short, complete—
    Then not too soon.

Yet still our tears will flow ;

We must have patience with the poor frail heart,

That cannot see afar, and feels to part

Is boundless woe ;

That has not faith's strong wings,

But in unutterable anguish yearns,

And ever to its earthly treasure turns,

And blindly clings.

And life to him was fair ;

All its best gifts for him were richly stored :

Wealth, happiness, and tender love were poured

All fondly there.

Ah ! we should say too soon,

Did we but listen to our treacherous heart.

God chose for Willie the " far better part "—

His last best boon.

The Half-Holiday.

A STORY FOR BOYS.

———•———

 HAPPY day is Wednesday,
    As all the boys can tell,
Who prize a holiday, and love
    The game of cricket well.

Eton and Harrow, Rugby,—all
    To fun are well inclined;
And Iver, equal in all else,
    Is not in this behind.

'Twas Wednesday, then,—a lovely day,—
   Cool was the pleasant air ;
The sun all smilingly shone forth,
   The glass was at " set fair,"

When out the boys from Iver school
   Sallied in wild array ;
Each beaming face, each bounding step,
   Proclaimed " half-holiday !"

Behold their earnest, active gait :
   No doubt the game is cricket,
For bats are shouldered gallantly,
   And Edward has the wicket.

What wild confusion, and what noise !
   Some laugh, some scream, some call ;
" Has any body brought the bails ?
   And who has got the ball ?"

To Guntsmore now they bend their steps
All hastily ; and hark !
That laugh and hearty shout announce
That they are in the park.

The owner of that fair domain
Has kindly said that they
Are welcome on his good green-sward,
Their merry games to play.

Yet oft it wonders me that he
His ground should thus have lent ;
For he must know that school-boys are
On mischief ever bent.

" But wise men are not always wise ;" *
And often we may find
Some failing or some weakness lurk
Within the strongest mind.

---

* " Nemo mortalium omnibus horis sapit."

An over-tenderness, which oft
  Around the kind heart clings,
Will make the wisest and the best
  Do many foolish things.

And some such weakness, doubtless, moved
  The heart of Mr Power;
He yielded to soft Nature's touch
  In an unlucky hour.

But, hark! the boys impatient grow;
  " Do let the game begin :
Come, Harrison, what *are* you at ?
  Let you and I pick in."

The sides are chosen, all are pleased;
  Their forces they review;
" We'll win," says Cameron, " for ours
  Are all ' good men and true.' "

" We've Herbert, and we've Harrison,
  Who is in bowling strong ;
We've Garnier for the back-stop,
  And Thompson for the long."

" Don't boast," says Dutton, " all our men
  To yours at least are equal ;
We'll show you all the way to win ;
  Wait till you see the sequel."

" Come on !" " Yet stay," says Perceval,
  " I will not long detain ;
Trotter, just lend me your new knife ;
  I'll give it you again."

" What you can want, now, with a knife,
  I cannot understand,"
Says Fred, but still, good-naturedly,
  He placed it in his hand.

Hard was the contest, and so well
  Each side its part maintained,
'T was long before a welcome shout
  Announced the victory gain'd.

And then the chattering all at once,
  Such boastings of the winnings ;
Such causes why the others lost,
  Such countings of the innings.

All the delight which battle-plains
  To knights and warriors yield,
Is theirs, who gallantly have won
  That " well-contested field."

" A jolly game ! I never had
  A better in my life ;
Give me my jacket ; let 's go home ;
  Percival, where 's my knife ?"

" Your knife ! oh dear, I quite forget ;
   Where is it ?   Let me see—
I had it, now I recollect,
   As I stood near that tree."

No common knife was this, I ween,
   As all the boys could say,
Who saw it when it first arrived,
   On Frederick's last birth-day.

A knife it *seem'd*, with two good blades,
   Just as its name profess'd,
But lo ! what properties besides
   This wondrous knife possess'd !

A hook, stiletto, gimlet, saw,
   In turns were brought to view ;
Pincers and tweezers, toothpick, and
   A capital corkscrew.

A very cutler's shop it seem'd,
 And gain'd great admiration ;
No wonder, then, its sudden loss
 Occasioned a sensation.

All cluster'd round the tree, all eyes
 Were peering on the ground,
And long they sought, but search was vain ;
 No knife was to be found.

Poor Perceval now ask'd " to think,"
 And now, " the place to show,"
Could only answer mournfully :
 " I'm sure I do not know."

This tree was large and hollow, and
 A hole within its side
Allow'd the prying eye to range
 Its cavern deep and wide.

And 't was remember'd, Perceval
    Just at the opening stood,
Cutting, in idle listlessness,
    Some portions of the wood.

" And don't you think, as that's the case,
    You might have dropp'd it then ?"
" I must, I think, have dropp'd it, but
    I'm sure, I can't tell *when.*"

Of " such strange absence of the mind,"
    They ne'er before had heard ;
" It must have fallen in the tree,"
    They one and all averred.

Yes, it was in that dark abyss,
    There could not be a doubt,
And the consideration next
    Was, how to get it out.

K

" 'Tis vain to peer into the dark,
    One cannot get a sight,
It is so gloomy all within ;
    I wish we had a light."

" A light ! a light ! yes that's the thing !
    Let's burn a piece of paper !
O nonsense ! that will never do :
    Has nobody a taper ?"

Contrivances are plentiful ;
    A light is found, and quick,
By active fingers, carefully
    'Tis fastened to a stick.

Then cautiously the torch is lower'd,
    And steadily it burns,
While every head of every boy
    Peeps in the tree by turns.

There lie display'd the wither'd leaves
　　Of many by-gone years ;
But of the lost unlucky knife,
　　Alas ! no trace appears.

" 'Tis gone, indeed !" and now the hope
　　Which had each boy inspired,
Like the exhausted torch first waned, ·
　　Then totally expired.

" Yes, it is gone ! our longer stay,
　　Or further search is vain ;
'Tis certain we shall never see
　　The birthday knife again !"

'Twas growing late, and towards their home
　　The baffled heroes sped,
And soon their murmurs and regret
　　Are calm'd and hush'd in bed.

Part Second.

'Tis night: her curtain nature draws
    Around the earth; on high
The stars peep forth, the pensive moon
    In beauty walks the sky.

She shines upon the village street,
    Silvering the old church tower;
She looks within the casements low,
    And cheers the midnight hour.

Radiant she smiles o'er Guntsmore park,
    Tinging the leaves with white;
And calm and still the mansion stands,
    Bathed in her lovely light.

How sweet the scene! how silently
　　Creation sleeps around ;
But, hark ! upon the startled ear
　　Breaks forth a sudden sound.

It scar'd the feather'd songsters all,
　　Within their leafy bower ;
It roused the deer in wild alarm ;
　　It wakened Mr. Power.

Again it comes, and louder still !
　　What strange unseemly riot
Invades the peaceful harmony
　　Of nature's holy quiet ?

Now many mingled voices rise,
　　The tumult draws more near ; ·
And speeding towards the mansion, see,
　　Two breathless men appear.

They leap the shrubs, they reach the house ;
    At once they loudly shout ;
Now lights are seen, a window opes,
    And then a head comes out.

'Tis Mr. Power, in angry mood,
    And spirits all perturbed,
Demanding who, at such an hour,
    His slumbers have disturbed.

With wild and hurried gestures, both,
    Regardless of his ire,
Exclaim, " O sir, within your park
    A noble tree's on fire !

All Iver's up, the engine's there ;
    But, sir, I greatly doubt,
Do what they will, it blazes so,
    They'll never put it out."

And so it proved ; their efforts all
    To quench the fatal fire,
Seemed only to increase the flame,
    And make it blaze the higher.

And fierce displeasure burned within
    The breast of Mr. Power ;
Indignant anger, just and stern,
    Upon his brow did lower.

" I'll know who did this wicked deed,
    Wait but the morning light ;
I'll teach the scoundrels how on me
    They dare to vent their spite.

" As I am magistrate myself,
    I can, with perfect ease,
Punish the rascals, one and all,
    Exactly as I please."

While Mr. Power still seeks the rogues,
  Inquiries still pursuing,
Turn we to Iver school, and see
  What our young friends are doing.

Ah! happy age, the glowing sun
  Which sheds his morning ray,
Commences not his daily course
  More cheerfully than they.

Within the spacious school-room, hear
  What mirth and wit abound,
And from the merry playground near,
  Laughter and noise resound.

Unconscious of the evil done,
  With spirits all elate,
They see, on horseback, Mr. Power
  Galloping to the gate.

Some idly their opinion give,
    " Think he is early out,"
While some, more curious, " wonder much
    What he has come about."

But soon a rumour, vague and strange,
    Excites surmises strong :
Whitmore, " believes all is not right,"
    Woodgate " that something's wrong."

Misgivings rise in every breast ;
    And on each earnest face
Both curiosity and fear,
    And anxious doubt, we trace.

And now in groups they whispering stand ;
    Says Muchell, " can it be
That, yesterday, we dropped a spark
    In that old hollow tree ?"

To say what really is amiss
   Kilcoursie " won't engage,"
But asks the nature of that place,
   In Iver term'd the " cage."

And now, assembled in the school,
   All anxiously they wait
From Mr. Chase's lips to learn
   Their greatly dreaded fate.

With awful brow the truth he states ;
   And then, in tone severe,
A dreadful catalogue of all
   Their many faults they hear,—

Their mischief, its enormity—
   He stops, for all the while,
Prodigious efforts he has made,
   To check a rising smile.

But come it *will*, the urchins quick
    The hopeful sign discern ;
And, freed from half their load of care,
    Venture to smile in turn.

And soon they learn that Mr. Power,
    Having with patience heard,
Exactly, every circumstance,
    And how the case occurred,

Has kindly said he will, *this once*,
    Their carelessness forgive
But hopes, 'twill prove a lesson, they
    Will think on while they live ;

Desiring only, that the men
    Who through the night have striven
To save the burning tree, should have
    Some compensation given.

The boys acknowledge the demand
    Is reasonable quite ;
Indeed, they inwardly admit
    The penalty is light.

Then straight dismissing every care,
    With spirits light and gay,
They laugh, and sport, and then discuss
    The question, " who's to pay ?"

Some jokingly on Frederick call,
    While some more justly say,
As Perceval occasioned all,
    He surely ought to pay.

Young Barlow laughingly declares
    " He thinks it is but right
The sum should be produced by him
    Who first procured the light."

Finch thinks "more reasonable far
   It surely is, that he ·
Should pay, who so imprudently
   Had poked it in the tree."

Then Mr. Floyd, in playful mood,
   Begs they will " silence keep,"
While he proposes every boy
   Should pay who got a peep.

But Fortune ever favoring rogues,
   Still these sad boys befriends,
Kind Mr. Chase has paid the whole,
   And so the matter ends.

" Hurrah !" cries Goodricke, and the shout
   Is echoed all around ;
" We've had a right good jolly spree,
   And Fred's new knife is found !"

Meanwhile, abroad the adventure spreads ;
. The villagers perplexed,
Shrugging their shoulders, all exclaim,
   " What will the boys do next ?"

What will they do ? we too may ask,
   'T were vain to prophesy ;
But if they study to be wise,
   And to their books apply,—

If they but diligently strive
   All knowledge to acquire,—
Why, who can tell, but some of them
   May " set the *Thames* on fire ?"

The Young Gray Head.

INTENSE grief has been known to turn the head gray in a few hours, to silver over in a single day the bright locks of the beautiful and the young. No doubt some of you, my young readers, will remember the sad history of the unhappy Queen of Scots, or the more recent and dreadful fate of the lovely and unfortunate Marie Antoinette, upon whom one night of unutterable grief did the work of years, and sprinkled her fair tresses with time's untimely snow. The tale I am about to relate is an humbler history, but one that I think will excite the sympathy of your young hearts, being both true and pitiful.

" Mother," said Allen to his wife, as he stood outside the cottage door, setting his teeth hard against the north wind,

" I am thinking that to-night, if not before, we shall have some wild weather ; it's brewing-up down westward ; and look, there goes a pair of sea gulls ; and such a sudden thaw.   If rain comes on, the water will rise.   That path by the ford is a nasty bit of road. Best let the children stay from school to-day.

" Do, mother, do, " said the two quick-eared little girls clinging to their father, and looking from his to the mother's face, but denial was there. "No harm will come to them," she said ; the mistress lets them out early these short days, and our Martha is so good and steady, that she may be well trusted to take care of herself and Lizzy too ; and so she ought, for she is a great girl, now, almost eight years old ; besides, they give the Christmas prizes at the school to-day."   The mother's will was law. She cannot err, thought Allen, so hugging his fair-haired Lizzy once more to his heart, and patting the demure little Martha's head, with a tender "God bless the darlings," went cheerily on his way to his daily toil.

There is something exceedingly touching in the look of early thoughtfulness, seen often on some childish little face among the poor, not the unnatural suffering of the factory child, but a staid quietness betokening in the depths of those young eyes a sense of life's cares without its miseries. The docile little Martha was one of this stamp; and now, proud of her age and the praise just bestowed by her mother, doubly attentive as wishing to justify her confidence, and holding Lizzy's hands, they stood,—and a lovelier pair was never sketched by paint-er,—the little one with large blue eyes and fair silken ringlets by the side of the nut-brown Martha, her smooth parted hair, sable and glossy as the raven's wing, and dark lustrous eyes full of serious yet innocent thought.

" Now mind and bring Lizzy safe home ; don't stop to pull a bough or berry by the way ; and when you come to cross the ford, be very careful ; that plank is so crazy, and the step-ping stones, if not overflowed, will be slippery ; but you are good children and steady as old folk,—I know I may trust you. " Thus warning and encouraging, Martha's gray cloak was tied lovingly on, and the mother's own warm shawl wrapt around little Lizzy. " Be sure to knot it tight like this when you come home, just leaving one hand free, to hold by ; and now one kiss and then away !" Ah, was there no sinking at that mother's heart as they turned to leave her, had she no foreboding of ill as she watched them down the lane, turning every now and then to give a loving smile, or shout another, "good bye, mother." Perhaps there was, for surely that day seemed unusually long and lonely.

Three miles lay between Allen and his cottage door that evening—and a rough and wet evening it was ; he had worked all day at a great clearing, stroke upon stroke, till his back ached and his arm dropped almost nerveless. But what did Allen care now, all was forgotten as he approached that dear and quiet resting-place, his home ; and there was a treasure hidden in his hat, a plaything for the children—a dormouse nest that he had found, the living ball coiled round for its long winter's sleep: and his thoughts, as he trudged stoutly on, was of Lizzie's shout of wonderment, and the quiet surprise in Martha's grave eyes, when by guesses and kisses they should win him to bring forth the little frozen captive. He has reached the lane, and there stands the dear cottage, the light streaming from the open door, warms him but to look at—and Sambo comes bounding to meet him with a short quick bark. But where are the tiny feet that always vied with Sambo's in their haste to greet him, the ringing voices,—like sweet silver bells,—and the soft little hands clasping each of his to lead him in in triumph ? His heart has sunk already. Who's flitting round the peat-stack in such weather ? "Mother, is that you ! where are the children ? have they come ?" The husky hurried answer was "No ! oh no !" To throw down his tools, hastily unhook the old cracked lantern, and while he lit it, speak a cheering word that almost choked him,—and was unheard by the distracted mother— was the work of a moment, and he was gone to where a fearful presentiment led him ; passing a neighbouring cottage in which he called for Mark to bear him company—for who could say what need there might be,—they struck into the path the children should take coming back from school, and many a call and shout was sent through the pitchy darkness ; and the lantern peered into every road-side thicket, hole, or nook, till suddenly something brushed past them—it was Sambo. " Hold the light low down ; he is making for the water. Hark ! I know that whine, the dog has found them."

So, speaking breathlessly, he hurried on towards the old crazy footbridge; but all that the dull contracted light could show was that it was gone; yet there was life somewhere more than Sambo's whine; a low sob came faintly on the ear, almost lost in the sobbing gust. Quick as thought, Allen leapt into the stream; he caught fast hold of something; the water was scarcely knee deep for a tall man; and half above it, propped by some ragged side piles, that had stopped endways the broken plank which had given way with the two little ones, clung Martha. There she crouched, with face white as a sheeted corpse, and rendered even more ghastly in the flickering light, with pale blue lips wide apart, and showing the pearly teeth, her eyes fixed like stone upon some object underneath; and, washed by that turbid water, one little arm and hand stretched out, and rigid, still tightly grasped her sister's frock. There lay Lizzie drowned! How could the doting father sustain that shock! Oh! the flinty rock cannot endure such blasting, as that soft, sentient thing, the human heart, is sometimes doomed to bear. They lifted her from her watery bed. Its covering gone, the graceful head hung like

a broken snow-drop, and one small hand that was free, too.
The mother's shawl was wrapped and tied according to the
last injunction, fast and warm, alas, too well obeyed, too fast ;
a fatal hold it had afforded to some rough crag that had
pinned her to the river's bed, while through the reckless
water her life's breath bubbled up. They had raised her
now, and parted the soft wet curls from her brow. To the cold
lips the father pressed his warm ones, ere they again wrapped
the shawl—now her winding sheet—around the precious clay.

From Allen's cottage all that night there shone a fitful
light : above and below, all were watchers there, save one
sound sleeper, for her parental care could avail no more—
but in the young survivor's throbbing brow and wandering
eyes delirious fever raged, and she would moan piteously
" Indeed, indeed, I kept fast hold—she won't move ! I tied
the shawl quite fast ! Oh, I am so weary ! She can't be
cold. If father were but here !" Broken sentences, but
showing the agony she had suffered. And lo ! when morning broke all bright, as if in mockery of their grief, a strange
sight was there ; that young head's raven hair was streaked

with white. Life struggled long with death in her small frame. She at length recovered, in part, and all went on as before. No! not as before—there was a vacant place in the cottage, a haunting memory in the heart, never to be filled or effaced.